BERRY

A NOTE TO PARENTS

Disney's **First Readers Level 3** books were developed for children who have mastered many basic reading skills and are on the road to becoming competent and confident readers.

Disney's **First Readers Level 3** books have more fully developed plots, introduce harder words, and use more complex sentence and paragraph structures than Level 2 books.

Reading is the single most important way a young person learns to enjoy reading. Give your child opportunities to read many different types of literature. Make books, magazines, and writing materials available to your child. Books that are of special interest to your child will motivate more reading and provide more enjoyment. Here are some additional tips to help you spend quality reading time with your child:

★ Promote thinking skills. Ask if your child liked the story or not and why. This is one of the best ways to learn if your child understood what he or she has read.

★ Continue to read aloud. No matter how old the child may be, or how proficient a reader, hearing a delightful story read aloud is still exciting and a very important part of becoming a more fluent reader.

★ Read together on a regular basis, and encourage your child to read to you often. Be a good teacher by being a good listener and audience!

★ Praise all reading efforts, no matter how small.

★ Try out the After-Reading Fun activities at the end of each book to enhance the skills your child has already learned.

Remember that early-reading experiences that you share with your child can help him or her to become a confident and successful reader later on!

— Patricia Koppman
Past President
International Reading Association

Pencils by Karen Rosenfield, Denise Shimabukoro, Orlando De La Paz

First published by Disney Press, New York, New York.
This edition published by Scholastic Inc.,
90 Old Sherman Turnpike, Danbury, Connecticut 06816
by arrangement with Disney Licensed Publishing.

SCHOLASTIC and associated logos are trademarks of Scholastic Inc.

ISBN 0-7172-6459-9

Printed in the U.S.A.

Parade Day

by Kathryn Cristaldi
Illustrated by Eric Binder and Christian Monte

Disney's First Readers — Level 3
A Story from Disney's
The Hunchback of Notre Dame

SCHOLASTIC INC.
New York   Toronto   London   Auckland   Sydney
Mexico City   New Delhi   Hong Kong   Buenos Aires

It was a beautiful, sunny day. But it wasn't just any day. It was Topsy-Turvy Day!

On Topsy-Turvy Day, everything in Paris was upside-down, inside out, wrong side up, or just plain backward.

And there was also a big, loud, happy Topsy-Turvy Day parade.

Up in the bell tower of Notre Dame, Hugo and Victor watched the noisy crowd below.

"Look, the happy people are gathering for the parade," said Victor.

"I hope there's lots of cool music," said Hugo.

Suddenly, a wonderful chiming sound
filled the air.
DING-DONG! DING-DONG!
"There's no sweeter sound," said Victor.
DING-DONG! DING-DONG!

"You make beautiful music, Quasi," said Hugo.

Quasimodo, the most famous bell ringer in all of Paris, smiled at his friends.

"But listen, Quasi," Victor started to say, "You'd better get moving—"

"Or you'll miss the Topsy-Turvy Day parade," Hugo finished.

Quasimodo loved parades. He knew how special today's parade was.

He also knew everyone did something fun in the Topsy-Turvy Day parade.

"What about me?" Quasimodo asked his friends. "I can't sing or dance or do anything in front of all those people. I'm too shy."

"Don't be shy," said a familiar voice.
It was Quasimodo's friend, Esmeralda.
"You are very special, Quasimodo. You'll
find something you like to do. You'll find
something you would like to share with
everyone. Then you'll forget all about being
shy." She took Quasimodo by the hand and
pulled him toward the stairs.

"Good-bye, my boy," said Laverne.
"Enjoy the parade," said Victor.
"Catch you later," Hugo called.

Quasimodo and Esmeralda headed into
the crowd.

"One, two, three, wheeee!!!" Esmeralda
sang. She twirled around her friend.

Esmeralda was a wonderful dancer.
Today she had planned a special dance just
for the parade.

"Come dance with me," said Esmeralda to her friend. "It's fun!"

Quasimodo closed his eyes. He began to spin. Faster and faster.

"Look at him go!" said a voice.

"Wonderful!" said another.

Quasimodo opened one eye. Uh-oh.
People were watching him. He fell down in
a heap.

"Don't worry, Quasimodo," said Esmeralda.
"I thought you were great."

Esmeralda skipped to the baker's shop.
"Look, Quasimodo," she giggled. "It's a
topsy-turvy cake." She pointed to a chocolate
cake. It was upside down. It had icing and a
cherry—on the bottom!
"Look at those cookies!" Quasimodo said.
"Yum!" said Esmeralda.
They went inside.

Quasimodo and Esmeralda bought two
cookies. The cookies were shaped like
apples. Quasimodo bit into his. "Hmmm,
this doesn't taste like an apple cookie," he
said. "And it has nuts on it."

Esmeralda bit into hers. "It's a topsy-turvy
lemon-nut cookie," she said.

Outside the bakery they heard a loud bark. A dog pranced through the crowd. It was pulling a man on a leash.

"Topsy-Turvy Day sure is fun," said Quasimodo.

"Fun is sure Day Turvy-Topsy," answered Esmeralda. They both laughed.

Just then a bird landed on Quasimodo's shoulder. It whistled a pretty tune.

"That's it!" said Esmeralda. "You could sing at the parade."

"La, la, la!" Quasimodo began.

"Tweet, tweet, tweet," sang the bird.

"Mee, mee, mee!" sang a man passing by.

"My, my, my!" sang a woman in a straw hat.

Quasimodo turned beet-red. "I can't sing in front of strangers," he whispered to Esmeralda. "I am too shy."

A man walked by, wearing a funny hat.
He was juggling three brightly colored balls.
"That looks like fun," said Quasimodo.
"I bet I can juggle, too."
He threw three oranges into the air.
"Oh, look! Two jugglers. Let's watch,"
said a little girl to her father.

PLUNK! PLUNK! PLUNK!
The oranges fell at Quasimodo's feet. How could he juggle with everyone watching?

Quasimodo and Esmeralda heard people laughing behind them. They turned around.

Two clowns tumbled through the crowd. One walked on his hands. The other did a cartwheel.

"Look at the silly clowns," said a little boy. He giggled and clapped his hands.

"Maybe I could be a clown," said Quasimodo.

He stood on his hands. Then he wiggled his feet in the air.

"Hooray!" shouted the little boy.

"He's good enough to join our act," said one of the clowns.

Quasimodo looked up. Everyone was cheering and pointing at him. He hid behind a fruit stand.

Esmeralda and Quasimodo passed a topsy-turvy puppet show.

They watched a puppet with a duck bill and rabbit ears chase another puppet with cat whiskers and a curly tail like a pig's.

"You won't find them in any barnyard," Quasimodo said.

"They are two mixed-up animals," Esmeralda agreed.

"Look, Quasimodo," said Esmeralda.
"It's the leader of the parade band."
BOOM! BOOM! BOOM! went his big
round drum.

"Maybe I could be a drummer," said
Quasimodo.

He picked up two old sticks and tapped
them on a wooden barrel.

THUD! THUD! CRACK! went his drum.

"That won't work," said Quasimodo.

"Don't you just love Topsy-Turvy Day?"
asked Esmeralda, clapping her hands.
"I can't wait to do my dance."
    She jumped high into the air and kicked
up her heels.

Quasimodo bit his lip. It was almost time for the parade. What could he do that was special? What could he do in front of a crowd? Why did he feel so shy?

"I wish I could do something," sighed
Quasimodo, "something that makes me feel
special, not shy."

Just then a horse pranced by. It wore a
fancy string of bells and beads.

JINGLE-JANGLE! went the bells.

Esmeralda's eyes opened wide.
"I've got it!" she shouted. "I know what you
can do!"

BOOM-TA-DA-DA-BOOM!
The band leader beat his drum. The
Topsy-Turvy Day parade was off!

Esmeralda twirled. The baker and the miller sang as they marched. The juggler tossed his bright balls high in the air. The clowns walked by on stilts.

And behind them all, right in step, was
Quasimodo. He held up a long string of bells.
RING DING-A-LING! RING DING-A-LING!
"What a wonderful sound!"
"What beautiful music!"
The crowd clapped wildly. But this time
Quasimodo did not mind. After all, he was
the most famous bell ringer in all of Paris.

Esmeralda danced back to her friend.

"I knew you could do it," she said. "You just had to believe in yourself."

Quasimodo looked at Esmeralda. He grinned. "I believe I have the smartest friend in the whole world!" he said.

Up in the bell tower of Notre Dame,
Hugo, Victor, and Laverne heard all the
chiming and cheering.

"Now that's the coolest kind of music,"
said Hugo.

"That's our Quasimodo," said Victor. "He
sure is something special!"

Enhance the reading experience with follow-up questions to help your child develop reading comprehension and increase his/her awareness of words.

Approach this with a sense of play. Make a game of having your child answer the questions. You do not need to ask all the questions at one time. Let these questions be fun discussions rather than a test. If your child doesn't have instant recall, encourage him/her to look back into the book to "research" the answers. You'll be modeling what good readers do and, at the same time, forging a sharing bond with your child.

1. In what city does the story take place?

2. Who was the most famous bell ringer?

3. Where did Quasimodo get the bells that he used in the parade at the end of the story?

4. Was there ever a time when you felt shy?

5. What does it mean when someone "turns beet-red"?

6. Tell what two words each contraction stands for: wasn't, you'll, I'm, don't, let's, they're.

Answers: 1. Paris. 2. Quasimodo. 3. he borrowed them from the horse. 4. answers will vary. 5. that person is blushing because he or she is shy or embarrassed. 6. was not, you will, I am, do not, let us, they are.